Mimi
the Laughter
Fairy

To Lowena and Iona

Special thanks to Rachel Elliot

ISBN 978-1-338-15769-7

10 9 8 7 6 5 4 3 2 1   17 18 19 20 21

Printed in the U.S.A.   40
First edition, July 2017

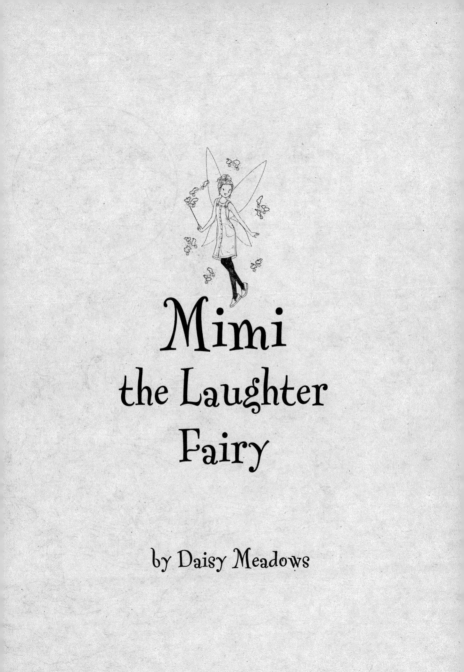

Mimi
the Laughter Fairy

by Daisy Meadows

SCHOLASTIC INC.

The Fairyland Palace

Stage

Palace Gardens

Rainspell Park

Tennis Court & Clubhouse

TENNIS

Sunny Days B & B

Rainspell Beach

The Friendship Fairies like big smiles.
They want to spread good cheer for miles.
Those pests want people to connect,
And treat one another with respect.

I don't agree! I just don't care!
I want them all to feel despair.
And when their charms belong to me,
Each friend will be an enemy!

Contents

Mr. Twinkle's Tumble

Kirsty Tate was spinning her way across the park, her arms outstretched as she soaked up the early morning sunshine. It was making the dew sparkle on each blade of grass, and it was shining on the golden hair of Kirsty's best friend, Rachel Walker.

"I wonder what Jen and Ginny have planned for us today," said Rachel, skipping along beside Kirsty.

It was their third day on Rainspell Island, the beautiful place where they had first met—and where they'd had their first fairy adventure! They were attending the Summer Friends Camp, a day camp for children staying on the island on vacation. The camp was held in the park every morning.

"We've already played soccer, had a water-balloon fight, and painted a mural," Kirsty remembered. "I'm so glad we've been going to camp."

They reached the tent where the camp was based and stepped inside. Oscar and Lara, two of their newest friends, dashed over to them.

"Good morning!" said Lara, a big smile on her face.

"Do you know what we're doing today?" Oscar asked.

"We have no idea," said Rachel with a grin. "But I think we're about to find out!"

Jen and Ginny, the teenage best friends who ran the camp, were beckoning everyone to gather around them. They looked as if they were about to burst with excitement.

"Today we have something really fantastic for you all to enjoy," said Ginny. "We're going to watch a special performance by Mr. Twinkle himself!"

Everyone gasped and squealed. Mr. Twinkle was the funniest, most famous magician on TV. Like all the others at the camp, Rachel and Kirsty watched his show every week.

"I can't believe we're actually going to see him *in real life*!" Oscar said in a breathless voice. "When I grow up, I want to be just like him and make everyone laugh!"

"Where's the performance going to be held?" Kirsty asked.

"Right here in Rainspell Park," said Jen with a smile. "We have to wait for him on the steps of the fountain square. I thought you could all race one another to see who gets there first. Ready? Set? Go!"

Everyone sped out of the tent and sprinted across the grass to the fountain in the middle of the park. A girl named Anouk won the race, and everyone gathered around to congratulate her.

Then they each found a place on the
steps to sit and wait for Mr. Twinkle.

"My heart's thumping," said Rachel. "I
don't know if it's because of running fast
or because I'm so excited!"

"There he is!" Kirsty exclaimed,
jumping to her feet.

Riding toward them on a unicycle was
a very strange-looking man. He was
wearing a long purple cape covered in
sparkly stars and a black top hat almost
as tall as he was!

"It's so amazing to see him in real life!"
said Rachel.

Mr. Twinkle waved at the children, his
sparkly cape flying out behind him and
a magic wand held high in his left hand.
The children clapped and cheered, but as
he reached them he started to wobble. He

zigzagged left and right, his arms waving wildly, but it was no use. *CRASH!* The unicycle shot into a nearby bush and Mr. Twinkle landed on his bottom, all tangled up in his magnificent cloak.

Rachel and Kirsty burst into laughter, but no one else seemed to think it was funny.

"He's better when he's on TV," Oscar said under his breath.

The other children had stopped clapping. Mr. Twinkle jumped to his feet, pulled off his hat, and swept a deep bow. Then he waved his magic wand over his hat and pulled out a flower.

"Look at this beautiful bloom!" he cried, holding it up in front of the children. "Take a sniff!"

Everyone leaned forward, and a stream of water squirted out of the flower and straight into their faces!

Rachel and Kirsty were helpless with giggles, but the other children still weren't amused.

"Why aren't you laughing?" Kirsty asked Lara.

"I'm not really in the mood for jokes," said Lara.

"I'm all wet," Oscar complained.

"It's only a few tiny drops of water," Rachel said, trying to make him see the funny side of it.

But Oscar and Lara shook their heads.

Rachel and Kirsty exchanged a worried glance.

"I have a terrible feeling that I know exactly why people aren't laughing," Kirsty whispered into her best friend's ear. "It's because of the Friendship Fairies' magical objects!"

A Gaggle of Grumblers

On the first day of their vacation, the girls
had met the Friendship Fairies. Esther
the Kindness had whisked them away to
a magical tea party in Fairyland with
her, Mary the Sharing Fairy, Mimi the
Laughter Fairy, and Clare the Caring Fairy.
Everything was perfect—until Jack Frost
and his naughty goblins had crashed the

party and stolen the Friendship Fairies'
magical objects. The Ice Lord had thrown
the objects to his goblins and sent them
to hide in the human world.

Rachel and Kirsty had managed to get
back Esther's heart brooch and Mary's
yin-yang charm, but two of the magical
objects were still missing.

As they watched everyone frowning
at Mr. Twinkle, Rachel and Kirsty knew
exactly why the other children didn't
feel like laughing. It was because Jack
Frost still had Mimi's magical smiley-face
pendant!

"The Friendship Fairies need their
magical objects to keep all friendships
strong and happy," said Rachel,
remembering what their fairy friends had
told them.

Kirsty nodded. "One of my favorite things about being best friends with you is laughing and having fun together. But until Mimi gets her pendant back, no one is going to find anything funny! Why does Jack Frost always have to be so mean?"

The girls looked back at Mr. Twinkle. He was still trying to make his audience laugh, but everything he did seemed to make them more grumpy.

"Jack Frost is only thinking about himself," said Rachel. "He ordered the goblins to find some friends for him, remember? He said that if he has lots of friends, he can boss them around and be super-powerful."

"But friends don't boss each other around," Kirsty said. "Oh, Rachel, thank goodness *our* friendship isn't being affected by the missing magical objects!"

Luckily, Kirsty and Rachel's friendship was protected by a "Friends through Thick and Thin" spell cast on their friendship bracelets by their old friend Florence the Friendship Fairy.

"Not yet," Rachel agreed. "But Florence said that the spell won't last long if the fairies don't get their objects back soon. We have to keep looking."

Just then, Mr. Twinkle raised his voice.

"I know what'll cheer you all up!" he exclaimed. "New clothes are always a treat. I'm going to make a brand-new tie for myself with magic. Get ready to be amazed, boys and girls!"

Mr. Twinkle waved his wand over the hat, but the wand suddenly flopped over like a piece of limp celery. With a confused expression, Mr. Twinkle pulled an enormous cream pie out of his hat instead of a tie.

"Now, that's not right," he said, scratching his head and looking puzzled.

Rachel and Kirsty doubled over with laughter, but the other children just shrugged. Jen raised an eyebrow at Mr. Twinkle, and he grinned at her.

"There's only one thing to do with a pie like this," he said. "It's just begging to be thrown! Cream pies are supposed to end up on people's faces."

He took one step toward her, and then another. He raised the pie and took aim.

"Don't you *dare*," said Jen, who didn't look amused at all.

She backed away, but Mr. Twinkle just kept coming toward her, faster and faster, until he was chasing her around in a wide circle. Rachel and Kirsty thought it was funny at first, until they saw how annoyed Jen looked.

"Stop it!" she shouted at him. "This is silly!"

Mr. Twinkle's shoulders slumped.

"But I *am* silly," he said in a miserable voice. "That's what I *do*. People usually love it."

"Not today," Jen snapped.

Mr. Twinkle put the pie down on the ground next to Rachel and Kirsty, climbed onto his unicycle, and rode away.

"Poor Mr. Twinkle," said Kirsty sadly.

The other children were busy
grumbling about how Mr. Twinkle wasn't
funny when Rachel noticed something
strange. The cream pie seemed to be
glowing. She leaned closer, and saw tiny
sparkles glittering on top of the cream.

"Kirsty," she whispered. "I think
something magical is about to happen!"

Goblin Antics

Rachel and Kirsty stood in front of the
pie so that none of the other children
could see what was happening. The girls
were always careful to keep the fairies a
special secret.

The cream at the center of the pie seemed
to lift into the air, and Mimi the Laughter
Fairy fluttered out from the middle.

Mimi was wearing a simple denim
overall dress with navy tights and
white shoes. A swirl of cream from the
cake was sitting
on top of her
reddish-brown
hair like a funny
hat. Cream had
also caught on
her shoulders
like a cozy cape,
and there was
even a dot of
cream on the
tip of her nose.

Rachel and Kirsty
couldn't help giggling.

"It's not funny," said
Mimi, looking annoyed.

The girls stopped laughing immediately, and Mimi sighed.

"I'm sorry," she said. "I'm the Laughter Fairy, but even *I'm* not laughing and keeping things light today. I have to get my magical smiley-face pendant back from the goblins before the Fairyland Funny Show tonight, but I have no idea how. Please, will you help me?"

Rachel and Kirsty nodded immediately.

"Of course we will," said Kirsty. "What's the Fairyland Funny Show?"

"It's usually one of the best nights of the whole year," said Mimi, looking anxious. "All the fairies tell jokes and perform tricks to make one another laugh, and the funniest fairy wins. But without my pendant, the show will be a disaster and friends will never laugh together again!"

Just then, Lara let out an excited yell
and pointed down the path. Three more
magicians were riding toward them on
unicycles. They were all dressed similar
to Mr. Twinkle, with green capes and
matching green top hats. They were
much more wobbly than Mr. Twinkle, and
they kept bumping their unicycle wheels
together and knocking one another off.

"I'd better hide," said Mimi, slipping into Kirsty's zippered pocket.

Rachel peered at the magicians as they got closer.

"They're wearing an awful lot of green," she said.

"Yes, and they have big feet and long noses," added Kirsty. She gasped. "Oh, Rachel—they're goblins! Do you think they might be the ones who have Mimi's pendant?"

"I bet they are," said Rachel. "That must be why they're dressed up like Mr. Twinkle—they want to make everyone laugh."

One of the goblins stood up on his unicycle, waving his arms as he tried to keep his balance. Another stood on his head and used his hands on the pedals. The third lay on his stomach with his arms and legs splayed out as if he were flying. They all looked so silly that even Rachel and Kirsty had to smile at their antics.

"Whichever goblin makes the other children laugh *must* be the one with Mimi's magical smiley-face pendant," Kirsty said.

But the other children were all still looking grumpy. The girls watched them closely, but they couldn't see even a flicker of a smile. Not one person was laughing.

One by one, the goblins jumped down from their unicycles and pulled out green magic wands.

"Now for some magic!" the tallest goblin declared. "Get ready, pesky humans—er—I mean, boys and girls!"

He waved his wand around his head and nearly knocked his hat off, but there was not a single giggle from the audience.

"Abracadabra!
Stinky-winky!
Fill this fountain
With a slimy green drinky!"

"That's a terrible rhyme," said Rachel.

"It's a terrible spell, too," Mimi added.

"Thankfully, it won't work. The goblins

don't know how to do magic."

The goblin was staring eagerly at the
fountain. When nothing happened, he
threw his wand down and jumped on it.

Next, the other two goblins held their
wands up in the air.

"On the count of three, we will cast
a spell to turn the trees into green
pom-poms!" the smallest goblin squawked.

"One . . . two . . . THREE!"

The goblins tapped their wands on one another's noses, and several green pom-poms dropped out from under their capes. The audience groaned.

"Booooo!" called Oscar.

"Cheaters!" Lara exclaimed.

"I can't understand it," said Kirsty.
"One of these goblins must be hiding
Mimi's magical object. But whoever has
the pendant should have the audience in
stitches!"

"Something must have gone wrong,"
said Mimi.

"Mimi, could you turn us into fairies?"
asked Rachel. "We'll have a better
chance of finding out what the goblins are
up to if we can keep out of their sight."

Jen, Ginny, and all of the other children
were still staring at the goblins, who were
now performing a strange dance routine
that involved kicking their legs up high
and banging their wands together as
hard as they could. No one saw Rachel
and Kirsty slip away to hide behind
the fountain. As soon as they were sure

that no one was watching them, Mimi
fluttered out of Kirsty's pocket and
tapped the girls with her wand. At once
they felt the familiar thrill of their wings
unfurling as they shrank to fairy size.
Suddenly, the world
seemed bigger and
brighter.

"Everything
looks a little
bit more
beautiful
when we're
fairies," said
Kirsty, twirling
around in a few
sparkling drops of
water that splashed
out from the fountain.

Rachel looked up at the fountain, too, and saw something interesting. There was a little platform at the top, almost hidden by the water that poured out around it.

"That's the perfect hiding place," she said. "From there, we might be able to see which goblin has the pendant."

Hand in hand, the three fairies zoomed up and perched at the top of the fountain. Through the tumbling water, they were able to see everything.

The goblins finished their show, but no one in the audience clapped. Looking angry, the goblins grabbed their unicycles and dragged them around to the other side of the fountain. They sat down on the dusty path and glowered at one another.

"That was a disaster," said the smallest goblin. "I blame Jack Frost."

"Me, too," said the middle goblin, pulling a stray green pom-pom from under his armpit. "If he hadn't taken that magical pendant from us, everyone would have been crying with laughter."

"I don't know why he wants it, anyway," added the tallest goblin. "Jack Frost doesn't *like* making people laugh."

Kirsty drew in her breath sharply.

"That's *it*!" she whispered. "I bet Jack Frost has taken the pendant because he wants to perform at the Fairyland Funny Show. If he has the pendant, everyone is sure to think he's the funniest act, and he'll win."

"And Jack Frost *loves* winning," Rachel said with a groan. "Mimi, there's no time to lose. Jack Frost is going to cheat, and that will ruin the whole show. We have to go to Fairyland and stop him!"

Bad Jokes!

Before Rachel had finished speaking, they arrived in Fairyland in a swirl of magical sparkles. They looked around and saw that they were in the garden of the Fairyland Palace. The lawn was dotted with picnic blankets and chairs where lots of fairies were sitting. They were all facing a little stage, complete

with a red velvet curtain. Mimi led
Rachel and Kirsty to stand in the left
wing of the stage just as the Showtime
Fairies ran onto the stage from the right.

"Welcome to the Fairyland Funny
Show!" cried Isla the Ice Star Fairy. "We're
so excited to present—WHOOPS!"

She squealed as she stepped on a
banana peel and skidded across the stage.
Madison the Magic Show Fairy grabbed
the microphone as Isla slid past.

"We've got jokes, sketches, and tricks," she announced. "But don't worry—I'm sure the whole show will go according to plan—OOOH!"

The microphone jumped out of her hand as if it were as slippery as soap! Rachel and Kirsty spluttered with laughter, especially because Isla was still sliding around on the banana peel behind Madison. One by one, the Showtime Fairies started to do cartwheels across the stage, but their legs got tangled until they all ended up in one great big cartwheel made of seven fairies.

It spun into the air and then twirled downward and landed with all the fairies *upside down.* The fairies flipped over backward and bowed—*with their backs to the audience.* Rachel and Kirsty howled with laughter and clapped until their hands were sore, but none of the fairies on the grass so much as smiled.

"No one's laughing," shouted a rough voice. "You're not funny."

Everyone looked around, trying to see who was shouting. Then a movement above the stage caught Rachel's eye. She gasped as she saw a huge, frosted-blue glitter ball coming down slowly, held by a thick chain. It was decorated with golden smiling faces. Two goblins were standing on top of the ball, clinging to the chain and wearing enormous

foam fingers.
One said,
"Jack
Frost is so
funny . . ." and
the other said,
". . . I can't stop
laughing!"
The goblins
were
giggling
hysterically,
their
cheeks pink
and their eyes
wet with tears of
laughter.

"*I'll* show you what's funny!" the rough
voice went on.

As the glitter ball
touched the
stage, it
opened
to reveal
Jack
Frost. He
stepped
out of the
ball, dressed in
a sparkly ice-blue cape and an enormous
sparkly blue top hat.

"It's me!" he announced.

To Rachel and Kirsty's amazement,
the audience roared with laughter. Mimi
drew in her breath sharply.

"Look what's around his neck," she
exclaimed. "My magical smiley-
face pendant!"

Jack Frost strutted across the stage, put his hands on his hips, and glared at the watching fairies.

"Knock knock!" he bellowed.

"Who's there?" they replied.

"Fairy," said Jack Frost.

"Fairy who?" the audience chanted.

"*Fairy* pleased to meet you!" he shouted.

Again the fairies squealed with
laughter, clutching their sides and rolling
around on the grass.

"How many fairies does it take
to screw in a lightbulb?" Jack Frost
demanded. "Three! One to screw it in,
one to cast a pointless spell on it, and one
to flutter around being annoying."

The fairies were crying tears of
laughter now. Jack Frost was on a roll.

"What do you call a fairy who's always
agreeing with you? Fairy Nuff! Get it?"

"These jokes aren't even *jokes*," said
Kirsty. "How can the other fairies think
they're so funny?"

"It's because he's wearing the magical
pendant," Mimi replied in a whisper. "As
long as he has it, every time he tries to be
funny, people will laugh. The only reason

I'm not laughing is because the pendant belongs to me. It can't be used to trick me."

"Why did the fairy cross the road?" Jack called out. "Because the silly thing forgot she could fly!"

The laughter was deafening, and a smug grin had appeared on Jack Frost's face.

"We have to get that pendant back *now*," said Rachel. "I can't bear to hear our friends laughing at these mean, unfunny jokes."

Suddenly, Kirsty grabbed Rachel's arm in excitement.

"I have an idea!" she whispered.

Pie Pandemonium

"Jack Frost thinks that he's the most amazing comedian ever," Kirsty said. "Let's pretend to be fans! He's so conceited that he's bound to believe us. We'll ask for his autograph, and then Mimi can unhook the pendant while he's signing."

"Great idea!" said Rachel.

The two friends started pretending to splutter with laughter, and they rushed onto the stage, swerved around the goblin assistants, and dashed over to Jack Frost.

"Your jokes are the funniest I've ever heard!" Kirsty gushed.

"Could we please, *please* have your autograph?" begged Rachel.

Jack Frost's smug smile grew even smugger. But then he looked at the audience and shook his head.

"I have a duty to *all* my fans," he said, putting his hand over his heart. "I must continue with the show, and you are interrupting me. Come back for an autograph later."

"But we can't wait," said Kirsty.

"Of course you can," said Jack Frost. "I'm the funniest, best, and most handsome act in all of Fairyland *and* the human world. You will wait until *I* am ready!"

He gave them both such a shove that they went skidding back into the wings, landing in a tangled heap of arms, legs, and wings. Mimi helped them up, and they all peered out on to the stage again.

One of the
goblin assistants
was doing
a wobbly
pirouette. As he
spun around, he
pulled a sparkly
blue wig from
behind the glitter
ball. The other goblin
did a little jig, then
dived into the glitter ball
and pulled out an enormous blue bow tie.

"Your outfit, sir," squawked the first
goblin.

Jack Frost snatched the wig and the
bow tie, and quickly put them on. Then
he swept a deep bow to the audience,
who were almost hysterical with laughter.

"Mr. Twinkle's bow tie is much better," said Rachel.

"So are his jokes," Kirsty added. "Remember the cream pie?"

She and Rachel grinned at each other, and then their eyes widened. They had exactly the same idea at exactly the same time!

"Mimi, can you use your magic to make a tray of cream pies?" Rachel asked.

Mimi just smiled and waved her wand. Instantly, a huge tray of whipped-cream pies appeared in Rachel's arms.

"Come on," she said to Kirsty. "We have to make Jack Frost *want* to give us the pendant!"

Rachel and Kirsty ran onto the stage and put the tray of pies down between them. Then they each picked one up and took aim.

"Three . . . two . . . one . . . FIRE!" Kirsty whispered.

WHOOSH! WHOOSH! Two cream pies flew through the air. *SPLAT!* One knocked Jack Frost's wig off. *SPLODGE!* The other was a direct hit right on his sharp nose, which poked through the paper plate.

Jack Frost yanked the plate off and clawed at his face, wiping great blobs of cream out of his eyes and flicking them onto the stage. The fairies in the audience were beside themselves, laughing even harder than before. They obviously thought that this was supposed to happen.

"Stop laughing!" Jack Frost snarled through gritted teeth. "This isn't part of my show! I'm the joke-*maker*, not the joke, you foolish wing-flappers!"

The laughter stopped immediately. Jack Frost turned to Rachel and Kirsty, his eyes blazing with anger. They stepped a little closer together. It made them feel braver to be beside each other.

"Give me those pies," Jack Frost hissed. "If anyone around here is going to be throwing cream pies, it'll be me, not a pair of crazy fairies."

"You can't have them," said Rachel, trying not to let her voice shake. "They belong to us, just like how that pendant you're wearing belongs to Mimi."

"Give them to me!" Jack Frost hollered. But the friends shook their heads.

"You can only have them if you give Mimi back her pendant first," said Kirsty. Jack Frost's eyes narrowed, and then he turned his head toward the audience. The girls could tell that he wanted more laughter and applause.

"They really liked it when you threw those pies," he muttered. "All right, if you insist. You can have the silly pendant—as long as I can throw some pies!"

A Lot of Laughter

Jack Frost took the pendant from around his neck and held it out to Rachel. She took it and flew to the wings, where she handed it straight to Mimi.

The Laughter Fairy hugged Rachel, and then darted onto the stage as Kirsty handed the tray of cream pies to Jack Frost. A grin spread across his face and he pointed to his goblin assistants.

"You!" he yelled. "Stand still!"

"No way!" squealed the goblins, darting sideways.

Cream pies flew through the air as the goblins dodged and weaved around the stage. Soon the stage floor was white and slippery with cream, and the goblins and Jack Frost were skating around in the mixture, staggering as they tried to keep their balance. The Music Fairies, who were in the audience, struck up a merry tune, and soon everyone was in fits of laughter. The goblins were doing everything they could to avoid being splatted, from climbing the stage curtains to doing the limbo under low-flying pies.

"Stand still!" Jack Frost shrieked again.

There was just one pie left. He started to chase the bigger goblin, but then he stepped on one of the sticky, splatted pies on the stage floor, and slipped on it.

"HEEELLLLP!" Jack Frost cried as he careered across the stage.

The pie he was holding flew high up into the air, and came down with the biggest *SPLAT* yet—right on top of his head! He landed on his bottom with a bump, and the whole audience roared with laughter.

Rachel and Kirsty hurried over to help Jack Frost to his feet. At first he looked furious, but as the applause rose and the audience cheered, he started to smile. Standing beside Rachel, Kirsty, and the two goblin assistants, he took several bows. The fairies rose to their feet and clapped their hands above their heads.

Jack Frost was looking happier than Rachel and Kirsty had ever seen him. He bowed again and again, soaking up the cheers and the applause. When the girls gave a final wave to the audience and headed back into the wings, the goblin assistants were still trying to drag Jack Frost off the stage.

"Please come," Rachel heard one of them begging. "We really need to get your costume into the washing machine before the cream pies stain it!"

Rachel and Kirsty grinned as they shared a hug with Mimi. Her pendant was safely hanging around her neck.

"Thank you both," said Mimi, beaming. "I am so happy to have my smiley-face pendant back, and it's all thanks to you. I have to send you home now, but I want you to know that I will never forget how you have helped me. Friends forever!"

The three of them shared a hug, and then Mimi waved her wand. There was a shimmer of fairy dust, and the laughter of the fairies faded. Rachel and Kirsty blinked, and saw that instead of the garden of the Fairyland Palace, they were once again standing beside the fountain in Rainspell Park. The laughter of the fairies had been replaced by the laughter of their friends in the Summer Friends Camp.

Mr. Twinkle was telling jokes, and Jen, Ginny, and all of the children were holding their sides and roaring with laughter. Even the goblins beside the fountain started giggling when Mr. Twinkle turned and squirted them with his water flower.

"It looks as if things are back to normal, thank goodness," said Kirsty, squeezing Rachel's hand.

Mr. Twinkle finished with an amazing trick where he made his hat disappear— and then reappear on Lara's head! Then, amid cheers, laughter, and claps, he rode his unicycle away down the path, waving good-bye.

"This has been the most fun day so far!" said Oscar as they headed back across the park to the tent.

Lara bent her knees and did a funny walk, setting everyone off into giggles again. Oscar started telling jokes, and Rachel and Kirsty glanced back at the fountain. The goblins were still beside it, watching the children and looking sad.

"No one should be left out," said Rachel, waving to the goblins. "Come and join us!"

Cheering up immediately, the goblins leapfrogged across the grass to catch up with the children. They tripped over their big feet and tumbled around, head over heels. Giggling, the other children joined in, leapfrogging over the goblins and one another. Their laughter rang out across the park, and Rachel and Kirsty exchanged a special smile.

"I'm so happy," said Kirsty.

"I know," said Rachel. "Now only Clare the Caring Fairy's magical object is missing. I hope we can get it back!"

"We will," said Kirsty determinedly.

"We won't stop until all friendships are as happy as ours!"

RAINBOW magic

THE Friendship FAIRIES

Rachel and Kirsty found Esther's,
Mary's, and Mimi's missing magic items.
Now it's time for them to help

Clare

the Caring Fairy!

Join their next adventure in this
special sneak peek . . .

The Last Day

It was a beautiful summer's afternoon
on Rainspell Island. Rachel Walker
shut the door of the Sunny Days Bed &
Breakfast behind her and skipped down
the steps. Her best friend, Kirsty Tate,
was waiting for her on the path, and
their parents had already started walking
toward the park.

"I'm really looking forward to this barbecue," said Rachel. "I'm starving!"

"I think the hot weather makes us hungrier than usual," said Kirsty with a grin. "Just *thinking* about burgers is making my stomach rumble!"

Rachel laughed and reached out to hold Kirsty's hand.

"This has been one of the best trips ever," she said as they hurried to catch up with their parents. "I can't believe that we're going home tomorrow."

"Vacations on Rainspell always go too fast," said Kirsty.

The two girls shared a secret smile. Rainspell Island was the place where they had met and become best friends, and where they had had their first adventures with the fairies.

"It's a great idea to celebrate the last day of the Summer Friends Camp with a barbecue," said Mr. Walker with a twinkle in his eye. "I love barbecues!"

At the start of their vacation, the girls had joined the Summer Friends Camp, a day camp for children who were staying on the island on vacation. Now that they had reached the end of their stay, it was time to say good-bye to all of their new friends.

"It actually has been harder to make friends than I thought it would be," Kirsty said to Rachel.

"I agree," Rachel replied. "It's all because of mean Jack Frost and his goblins. They've caused a lot of trouble."

Walking a short distance behind their parents, the girls talked quietly about the adventures they had been sharing with the Friendship Fairies over the last few days.

"It's been nonstop magic since the day we arrived," Kirsty remembered. "Esther the Kindness Fairy whisked us off to Fairyland for a tea party with her and the other Friendship Fairies."

"It was wonderful until Jack Frost turned up," Rachel added.

Jack Frost and his goblins had sneakily stolen the fairies' magical objects while no one was looking. He wanted to use them to get lots of friends that he could boss around. And, as long as he had the magical objects, friendships in the human and fairy worlds would suffer.

"Jack Frost loves trying to ruin everyone's fun," said Kirsty. "This time he's made it really hard for friends to get along. Even Jen and Ginny have argued a few times."

Jen and Ginny were the teenage best friends who ran the Summer Friends Camp.

"Thank goodness that Florence the Friendship Fairy cast a 'Friends through Thick and Thin' spell on our friendship bracelets," said Rachel. "I can't imagine ever fighting with you. It would be horrible!"

Kirsty smiled, but she still looked anxious. Ahead, her parents were laughing with Rachel's parents. Even their friendships would be ruined if Jack Frost could not be stopped.

RAINBOW magic

Which Magical Fairies Have You Met?

- ❏ The Rainbow Fairies
- ❏ The Weather Fairies
- ❏ The Jewel Fairies
- ❏ The Pet Fairies
- ❏ The Sports Fairies
- ❏ The Ocean Fairies
- ❏ The Princess Fairies
- ❏ The Superstar Fairies
- ❏ The Fashion Fairies
- ❏ The Sugar & Spice Fairies
- ❏ The Earth Fairies
- ❏ The Magical Crafts Fairies
- ❏ The Baby Animal Rescue Fairies
- ❏ The Fairy Tale Fairies
- ❏ The School Day Fairies
- ❏ The Storybook Fairies
- ❏ The Friendship Fairies

SCHOLASTIC

HIT entertainment

Find all of your favorite fairy friends at
scholastic.com/rainbowmagic

RMFAIRY17